CW00869425

For Erika and Albus

Published by HRP Publishing
Text and illustrations copyright © Helen Rygh-Pedersen 2020
ISBN: 978-82-93831-04-4

The author / illustrator asserts the moral right to be identified as the author /
illustrator of the work. All rights reserved. No part of this publication may be
reproduced, stored in a retrieval system, or transmitted in any form or by any means,
electronic, mechanical, photocopying, recording or otherwise, without the prior
permission of the author / illustrator.

HRP
PUBLISHING

A Whiff in the Woods

Written and illustrated by
Helen Rygh-Pedersen

On Little Skunk's first
day at school
he washed and
groomed and hoped
he looked cool.

But deep
down inside
he really
was scared
that his
shameful secret
soon would be
shared.

His mum
turned to go
and he begged
her to stay.
"Don't be
silly," she said.
"Now, go and
play."

He joined the group and
began to smile,
for they ran and played for
such a long while.

They jumbled and
frolicked, tumbled
and skipped...
but in all the fun,
Little Skunk

LET RIP!

He stopped in his tracks and his face turned grey:

his

STINKIEST

secret came out with a spray!

His new friends puffed, spluttered and coughed:
Deer even stuck his head in the trough!
They each held their breath and their cheeks went pink
all because of his

stink.

"Come back," Skunk said. "I
want to play."
"You SMELL," they gasped.
"GO AWAY!"

So Little Skunk ran, his head
in his hands.
"Why must I smell? I don't
understand!"
He sat on a log and he cried
great big tears,
embarrassed by what he
had done near his peers.
"I just wanted friends, but
it's not meant to be.
I wish I was ANYONE ELSE
except me."

The next day at school he played on his own
and Teacher sat him in a 'SKUNKS-ONLY' zone.

Although she smiled kindly, she backed away too,
looking at him like he'd just stepped in poo.

At the end of the day, as he turned to head back,
a roaring machine felled a tree with a

CRACK!

Panic broke out and his
classmates flew past.
They screamed out in terror
and ran really fast.
Skunk turned to look but was
frozen in fear
as he saw bright white lights
and big tyres appear.

The monster machine was ploughing down trees, crushing up plants and scrunching up leaves.

All Skunk could do was sit there
and quiver,
when suddenly, the loggers
crossed over the river!

He dived in a bush and gazed on, aghast,
shaking with fear as the truck rumbled past.
He was scared he would die. He felt like
a coward...

...when out burst a stink that was

Little Skunk shocked himself and was struck quite dumb
when the loggers retreated, all thanks to his bum.
They gagged and they retched and one shouted "Quick!
Pass me a bucket. I'm gonna be sick!"
Away they all ran from Skunk's powerful smell,
falling over their feet with screams and a yell.

From out of the bushes, his friends reappeared.
They clapped him and hugged him and let out
three cheers.
"Our hero!" they shouted. "Skunk saved the day,
and all because of your stinky spray!"
Skunk was delighted: he had friends at last
and the shame of his smell was now in the past.

They partied all day, and they played lots of games.
Things in the forest were not quite the same, but his classmates were safe now and wanted to know:
what would happen if Skunk let one go...?

Little Skunk chuckled and gave a big grin.

"I promise from now on: I'll face downwind."

Lightning Source UK Ltd.
Milton Keynes UK
UKHW050330270121
377673UK00001B/2